the Legend of
SIR MIGUEL

the Legend of

SIR MIGUEL

written and illustrated by
MICHAEL CAIN

LANDMARK EDITIONS, INC.

P.O. Box 4469 • 1402 Kansas Avenue • Kansas City, Missouri 64127
(816) 241-4919

Dedicated to the ones who
have touched my life so deeply:
my parents, Gary and Patricia Mason;
my grandparents;
my teachers, past and present;
all my friends;
and the staff of Landmark Editions.
Without their love and support,
this book would not have been possible.

Second Printing

COPYRIGHT © 1990 BY MICHAEL CAIN

International Standard Book Number: 0-933849-26-5 (LIB.BDG.)

Library of Congress Cataloging-in-Publication Data
Cain, Michael, 1977-
    The legend of Sir Miguel / written and illustrated by Michael Cain.
    p.   cm.
    Summary: Miguel, aspiring to become a knight in armor, goes on a quest after
the oval crystal of Merlin, the only amulet that can save the kingdom from the spells
of the evil witch Dorinda.
    ISBN 0-933849-26-5 (lib. bdg.)
    1. Children's writings, American.
    [1. Knights and knighthood — Fiction.   2. Fantasy.
    3. Children's writings.]
    I. Title.
PZ7.C1195Le   1990   [Fic] — dc20   90-5927
                                                   CIP
                                                   AC

Editorial Coordinator: Nancy R. Thatch
Creative Coordinator: David Melton

Printed in the United States of America

Landmark Editions, Inc.
P.O. Box 4469
1402 Kansas Avenue
Kansas City, Missouri 64127
(816) 241-4919

329283

THE LEGEND OF SIR MIGUEL

Michael Cain was determined to win The National Written & Illustrated by... Contest. When the book he entered in the 1988 Contest did not win, he wrote and illustrated an even better book and was a winner in the 1989 Contest.

"If THE LEGEND OF SIR MIGUEL had not won," Michael told me, "I would have created another book for the 1990 Contest."

We see this type of determination in most of our winners. They are goal-oriented young people who are willing to rewrite their manuscripts and redo their illustrations until they feel they have done their very best work.

When Michael is writing or drawing, he offers his work one-hundred-percent concentration. There seems to be a special magnetism between Michael and the paper before him. Ideas come quickly to him. And he will spend the necessary time to expand those ideas into written words or beautifully composed illustrations. I enjoyed discussing improvements for illustrations with Michael. His eyes were so expressive that I could see the images take form in his mind. It was a spooky and wonderful experience to then see those same images unfold in his preliminary drawings.

In the LEGEND OF SIR MIGUEL, Michael has created a glorious tale of knights in rusted armor, a beast in a forest, an ancient wizard, a spellbinding witch, and a young man's quest to prove his courage and become a knight. As the adventure quickens and the excitement builds, Michael's brilliant illustrations illuminate the pages with a panorama of color and action.

Let the quest begin!

— David Melton
Creative Coordinator
Landmark Editions, Inc.

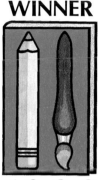

WINNER

1989
WRITTEN &
ILLUSTRATED
BY... AWARD

the Legend of SIR MIGUEL

As a young man, I, Miguel of Sheltingham, traveled to the Castle of Nor with the hope of becoming a great knight. I was eager to display my skills with the sword and lance. I longed to don my armor and ride my trusted steed into the heat of battle. I dreamed of performing heroic deeds and challenging impossible odds.

But, alas, my chance of becoming a knight seemed slight indeed. It had been my great misfortune to be born years too late. All the great battles had already been won. All the dragons had been slain. All the knights had retired. And all the wizards had died, except for one — Melchior the Magnificent.

Melchior, or the Ancient One as he was often called, lived in the north tower of the castle. It was said that he had been the last student of the Great Merlin. Now that Merlin was gone, it was believed that Melchior alone possessed the knowledge of certain magical spells and secret potions.

But Melchior had not been seen for many years because he no longer came out of his chambers. And no one dared to ascend the stone steps to the north tower, for it was rumored that Melchior might transform intruders into lowly toads. But one heard so many rumors within the castle walls that it was impossible to know which ones to believe.

Once a week the old wizard's manservant, Olaf the Dwarf, left the wizard's chambers and shuffled down the steps to gather a fresh supply of food and herbs. At such times I often stationed myself in the hall near the tower. When the dwarf passed my way, he never spoke or even glanced in my direction. But I sometimes dared to look up the stairs, hoping to get a glimpse of the Ancient One. I was curious to see the old wizard, for it was said he had lived for more than one hundred years.

On other days I would go to the Great Hall where King Ansel held court. Anyone who had a problem was welcome to come there and ask the king's advice. One Friday a group of villagers hurried in to tell him about a problem that could place everyone in danger.

"Your Majesty," one villager exclaimed, "there is a terrible beast in Galwin Forest!"

"What kind of beast?" King Ansel inquired.

"A horrible monster!" the villager replied. "It is twice as big as any man."

"Has anyone else seen this beast?" the king asked, looking about the room.

"We have seen it too," the others joined in.

King Ansel was greatly disturbed by the news. "I will summon my gallant knights of yore," he announced. "They will come and rid Galwin Forest of this beast."

That very day messengers were sent forth to the great knights of the kingdom, entreating them to journey with haste to the castle.

As I waited for the knights to arrive, I was beside myself with excitement. I had heard many stories of their bravery, and I was eager to see these legendary men. I even hoped that I might be allowed to accompany them in their search for the beast. If I proved my courage against such a monster, perhaps I, too, could become a knight.

When the trumpeters signaled the approach of riders, there was a rush of excitement. Everyone hurried into the courtyard to greet the knights. I made my way to the front of the crowd.

As the first knight entered the castle gate, it was difficult for me to hide my disappointment. He was not the bold warrior I had expected to see. He was an old man — frail and weak. And his armor was not polished and shiny. It was dented, rusted, and tarnished with age.

I watched sadly as the knights filed into the courtyard. Each one appeared to be older than the one before him. With great effort the twelve old men dismounted and formed a line before King Ansel.

"We are at your command, Sire," said Sir Aleron, leaning against his lance for support.

"Ride forth, great knights, to Galwin Forest and slay the beast that frightens my people!" the king ordered.

Before the knights could turn to leave, I brazenly stepped forward.

"Please, Sire," I pleaded, "allow me the honor of riding beside these noble knights. I, too, wish to prove my courage in the face of danger."

"Only if they approve," the king said.

To my great disappointment, all twelve knights shook their heads and said, "No!"

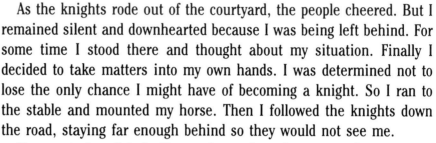

As the knights rode out of the courtyard, the people cheered. But I remained silent and downhearted because I was being left behind. For some time I stood there and thought about my situation. Finally I decided to take matters into my own hands. I was determined not to lose the only chance I might have of becoming a knight. So I ran to the stable and mounted my horse. Then I followed the knights down the road, staying far enough behind so they would not see me.

Upon entering Galwin Forest, I urged my horse to a faster gait. I did not want to lose sight of the other riders. Tree branches grew so thick they blocked out most of the light of day. And the farther I rode, the darker and more frightening the forest became. I wrapped my cloak around me to protect myself from the chill wind that moaned through the branches.

Suddenly our horses were startled by the noise of *someone* or *something* running past us.

"There's the beast!" one knight cried out. And the chase began.

"Now it's over here!" another knight called. And we headed in the opposite direction.

When I saw a dark shadow run past me, I turned my horse and raced after it. But as quickly as I had seen the creature, it was gone.

Although we looked for the beast all day, we could not find it. By late afternoon the old knights had tired of the search and decided to return to the castle. But I remained. I was determined to find the beast. So I continued to ride deeper and deeper into the forest.

I heard a roll of thunder, and drops of rain began to fall. As I looked for shelter, a bolt of lightning struck a tree in front of me. My startled horse reared up and threw me to the ground. I must have hit my head on a rock because everything went black.

The events that followed are still unclear to me. However, I do remember *someone* or *something* lifting me from the ground and carrying me in its strong arms for some distance.

When I finally regained my senses, I raised my hand to my face and discovered a bandage wrapped around my head.

"Are you feeling better?" a voice asked.

I opened my eyes and saw the beast standing over me. He was a frightful thing to behold. His shoulders were mammoth, and he was nearly twice the size of a man. He had long ears, and his face was covered with hair.

"How long are you going to keep me your prisoner?" I asked.

"You may leave as soon as you're well enough to travel," the creature assured me. "I mean you no harm."

"Then why do you attack others who come to the forest?"

"I do not attack them," the beast explained. "I only try to keep them away from the spring. But they are frightened by my appearance, and they run away."

"Why don't you want them near the spring?"

"Because there is something evil in the water," he replied. "It has the power to cast magic spells."

"How do you know that?" I asked.

"I know because a spell was cast over me," the beast said sadly. "I used to be a woodcarver by trade. Last summer I came to the forest to select the finest wood for my work. By the time my donkey and I reached the spring, we were very thirsty. We began to drink the cool water. But as soon as I took one mouthful, I fell into a deep sleep. When I awakened, my donkey was gone and I no longer looked like a man. I had become this hideous creature you see before you."

As the beast told his story, tears fell from his eyes and rolled down his furry cheeks. "I fear I am doomed to look like this for the rest of my life," he cried. "And I can never return to my wife and children. So I stay here and scare others away from the spring. I try to protect them from being changed into horrible creatures too."

"That's a noble thing for you to do," I said.

"I miss my family," he wept, hiding his face in his hands. "The loneliness I feel is the greatest pain I have ever known."

"What is your name?" I asked.

"Jonathan," he replied.

"Well, Jonathan," I said, "I think I know of someone who may be able to reverse the curse. There is an old wizard in the castle who knows all about magic and evil spells."

"Do you think you can persuade him to help me?" Jonathan asked.

"I will try," I promised.

As soon as I had regained my strength, I returned to the castle. Mustering all the courage I could, I went straight to the north tower and ascended the stone steps. When I came to the entrance of the wizard's chamber, I stopped and took a deep breath. Then I grasped the huge iron ring and banged it against the door. Soon I heard the grating of metal bolts being slid from their casings. Then slowly, very slowly, the massive door creaked open. In the musty darkness, Olaf the Dwarf stood before me.

"I've come to see the Ancient One," I said as boldly as I could.

"It is not allowed," the dwarf replied sternly.

"But I think the wizard will want to know about the strange things that are happening at the spring in Galwin Forest. People who drink its waters are turned into beasts."

Olaf considered my words for a few moments. "Wait here," he finally ordered and then shuffled out of sight. When he returned, he pulled the door wide open.

"Melchior the Magnificent will see you now," he announced. "You may enter."

When I stepped into the dimly lighted chamber, I was fascinated by the sights and sounds. The dusty shelves were full of books, glass jars, and cages. And strange potions bubbled and gurgled in ghostly beakers on the table.

Through the dimness I saw the Ancient One sitting in a hand-carved chair of enormous size. He was very old indeed. His white beard was so long it touched the floor. His bony hand clutched a crooked staff. And a black cat with blue eyes purred contentedly on his lap.

"What is this about the spring in Galwin Forest casting evil spells?" he asked impatiently.

"It has already turned an innocent woodcarver into a beast!" I replied.

"I thought all of that had been settled years ago!" the wizard said angrily and hit his fist on the arm of the chair. "Now I will have to return to the spring. I must go at once!"

Olaf and I helped Melchior to the door and down the stone steps to the courtyard. The dwarf saddled two horses. We gently lifted the wizard onto his horse and Olaf climbed up on the other one. As they followed me to Galwin Forest, Olaf rode close to the old wizard's side to make sure his master did not fall.

When we reached the edge of the forest, Melchior stopped his horse and said, "I can feel it now, but it is more powerful than I had expected."

"What do you feel, Master?" Olaf inquired.

"The evil," replied Melchior. "Its strength is growing at an astounding rate. I hope we are in time to put a stop to it."

We found Jonathan waiting for us by the spring. As Olaf and I helped Melchior down from his horse, Jonathan stepped forward and spoke to the wizard.

"Please tell me, Sir," he said, "can you free me of this evil spell?"

"I don't know," Melchior replied. "It depends on how strong the evil has grown."

We watched as the Ancient One slowly made his way to the spring.

"This is the place it happened," he told us. "This is where Merlin drove the evil witch, Dorinda, into the core of the Earth. She was the most wicked of all witches. Her evil was stronger than that of all the others put together."

Then Melchior turned and faced the bubbling waters. He leaned forward and looked deep into the dark hole that spiraled downward in the center of the spring.

"Just as I thought," he said, shaking his head in dismay. "Dorinda is alive. She is regrouping her powers to take over this kingdom and beyond. I will call her forth."

Reaching into the pouch that hung from his waistband, Melchior brought out a handful of golden powder and threw it into the spring. The water immediately began to foam and swirl, and a spire of mist rose before our eyes. We watched in amazement as Dorinda appeared in the center of the mist. But she didn't look as I had expected. I thought she would be an ugly old hag.

"Why, she's beautiful!" I exclaimed.

"So she appears," Melchior replied. "But Dorinda uses her beauty to beguile. Just remember, beyond the loveliness of a rose are sharp and painful thorns. And within Dorinda's twisted heart dwells the worst of evils. We must find a way to stop her!"

"You do not have the power to stop me, old wizard," Dorinda laughed.

"Careful!" Jonathan warned. "She may step out of the mist and kill us all."

"This is not Dorinda you see," the Ancient One explained. "It's only an image of her that I have conjured from my mind. The real Dorinda is still held captive in the core of the Earth. But not for long, I fear."

"Soon, *very* soon," the image sneered, "my powers will be strong enough to destroy all of you!"

Upon hearing that, the wizard commanded, "Be gone!" And the spire of mist disappeared into the water, taking the image of Dorinda back into the depths of the spring.

For some time the old wizard stood in silence.

"Can you stop her?" I finally asked.

"Not alone," he replied. "Such a feat will require the powers of a wizard of the magnitude of Merlin. I must consult with him."

"But I thought Merlin was dead!" I exclaimed.

"He is not dead. He has only passed to another dimension," Melchior replied. Then placing his hand to his forehead, he thought aloud, "Now let me see. I used to have a special incantation for contacting the Great Merlin, but I fear I have forgotten it. Oh, well, it makes no difference anyway. It didn't work the last time I tried it. There is only one method that truly works — the *Pyre of Fire.*"

Then turning toward us, Melchior commanded, "You and Jonathan start cutting wood — enough wood to melt the walls of a blazing furnace. Stack it here in the center of the clearing. Do it quickly! Our time is short!"

Jonathan and I did as we were told. While we chopped limbs from trees and carried the heaviest logs, Olaf gathered lighter branches. Together we piled, stacked, and layered a towering pyre.

When we had finished, Melchior reached up and pulled a ball of fire out of the air. With a wave of his hand, he threw the blazing orb into the tower of wood. The pyre burst into flames.

"You must keep this pyre burning for three days and three nights," the old wizard instructed. "If you value my life, you must maintain the fire at its hottest pitch." Then, to our surprise, Melchior turned and stepped into the fiery inferno.

It was difficult for Jonathan and me to believe that the old wizard could walk into such intense flames and live. But we realized there was much about magic that was beyond our understanding. So on faith alone, we continued to cut more logs and throw them into the flames. At night we took turns sleeping so that one of us could feed the raging fire.

Toward the close of the third day, Olaf suddenly stopped gathering branches and stood quietly before the flames. In a matter of moments, Melchior stepped out of the burning pyre. Olaf handed his master a flask of water, and the wizard eagerly drank his fill.

"I have conversed with the Great Merlin," the Ancient One finally said. "Together we have looked into the future of what the world could become. We have seen things that would astound your imaginations — ships that fly through the sky on metal wings and medicines that cure all ills.

"The world is ready to embark on a new age of science and reason. But if Dorinda's powers are allowed to be unleashed, the people of the world will be held captive in ignorance and superstition. Merlin says she must be stopped at any cost!"

"Will Merlin help us?" I asked.

"He cannot," the Ancient One replied. "Since Merlin now resides in another dimension, he can no longer alter events in this world. But he has offered wise advice."

Melchior raised his hand and pointed toward the setting sun. "A full day's ride to the west," he said, "is the Desert of Salazar. Beyond is a range of tall mountains. On the peak of the highest mountain, the Giant Peridrone guards her nest. In ancient times there were many of her species. But now they are all gone, except for this lone survivor.

"The Giant Peridrone fiercely protects her nest because she thinks it holds the last egg of the peridrones. She believes the egg will one day hatch and her fledgling will take her place. But she is wrong. Merlin has fooled her. Shortly before he passed into the other dimension, he removed the peridrone's egg and replaced it with his oval crystal. He knew the peridrone would shield it from all harm.

"The oval crystal contains the source of great magic," the wizard explained. "If we are to destroy the powers of Dorinda, someone must journey to the nest of the Giant Peridrone and bring the crystal to me."

"I will go!" I offered boldly.

"Very well, young man," Melchior replied. "But I must warn you of the danger you face. The talons of the Giant Peridrone are as sharp as razors. Take Jonathan with you. You are likely to need his help."

"We will prepare to leave at daybreak," I said.

At sunrise we rode forth on our journey. We traveled west to the edge of the forest, then made our way across the desert flats. By noon the sun burned high in the sky.

By riding day and night, we finally neared the mountains toward the end of the third day. We watched as the sunset created a palette of colors in the western sky. When darkness came we rode by moonlight until we reached the base of the tallest mountain. There we fed our horses, ate our own rations, and fell into an exhausted sleep.

Jonathan and I awakened as the dawn of the new day sent forth its first rays of light. When the sun crept above the horizon, the fog that rolled around the cliffs like dancing spirits soon disappeared.

Suddenly our horses whinnied and shied nervously. When Jonathan and I looked up, we saw the Giant Peridrone extend her enormous wings and circle in the morning sky.

Melchior had been right. The peridrone was unlike any bird we had ever seen. Horns protruded from her crested forehead. Her neck was covered with leathery scales. And her wings bore fanglike tusks. Even from such a distance, we could see her razor-sharp talons glistening in the sunlight. We watched in fascination as the peridrone rose on the currents of wind and flew away in search of prey.

I knew that Jonathan was as frightened as I, but neither of us suggested turning back. Without saying a word, we took ropes from our saddles and began to climb the jagged face of the mountain.

Our plan was a simple one. While the giant bird was away scavenging for food, Jonathan and I would remove the crystal from her nest. If luck was with us, we would have the crystal and be gone before the peridrone returned. But everything was not to go as we had planned.

When we finally reached the top of the mountain, Jonathan and I hurried to the peridrone's nest. There in the center lay the oval crystal. I was glad Jonathan was with me because the crystal was larger and much heavier than I had imagined.

Wasting no time, we made a sling out of my cape, rolled the crystal onto it, and tied the corners securely with a rope. Together we lifted the sling and carried it to the edge of the cliff. Holding tightly to the rope, we began to lower the crystal down the mountain.

Suddenly we heard an angry squawk. We looked up and saw the Giant Peridrone flying straight toward us! Knowing Jonathan had the strength to manage the crystal alone, I let go of the rope and sprang into action. I unsheathed my sword and prepared to do battle. The angry peridrone swooped down at me with her claws extended, ready to slash me to ribbons. I swiftly dodged to the side before she could strike.

"It's almost down," Jonathan called out.

The peridrone attacked again. This time she came so close I could feel the heat of her foul breath. By quickly dropping to my knees, I managed to avoid her razor-sharp talons.

"The crystal is on the ground," Jonathan called.

"Then climb down now!" I yelled to him. "Don't wait for me!"

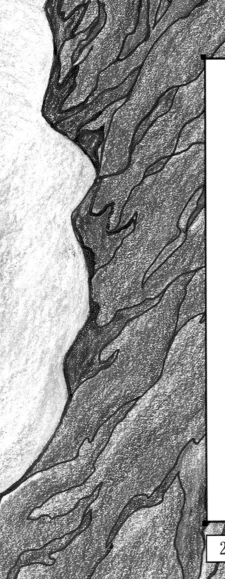

As the peridrone sped past me once more, I swung my sword and nicked her wing. But her bladed claws slashed across my right shoulder and spun me toward the cliff's edge.

While struggling to regain my balance, I noticed Jonathan had not started to climb down the mountain. Instead, he had lifted a stone that was similar in size and shape to the oval crystal. I watched in surprise as he raised it over his head and threw it into the nest.

The Giant Peridrone had seen Jonathan too. Screeching and hissing, she dove at him at full speed, snatched him in her claws, and lifted him into the air. I leaped forward and ran my sword into her leg. She let out a piercing scream and dropped Jonathan to the ledge below. Then she soared upward with the blade still lodged in her leg.

I tried to climb down before the peridrone could attack me too. But I didn't move fast enough. She hit me and sent me tumbling backward. As she turned skyward, I scrambled behind some boulders and hid.

While the peridrone continued to squawk and circle above me, I leaned forward and looked down the mountainside. To my relief, I saw Jonathan load the crystal onto his horse and start across the desert. I wanted to join him, but with the peridrone hovering overhead, I dared not try to escape. Without a weapon to defend myself, I knew I would be easy prey for the terrible bird. All I could do was wait and watch.

To my amazement, the peridrone soon stretched her wings and glided home to her nest. She grabbed hold of my sword with her beak and pulled the blade from her leg. Then she tossed the weapon out of the nest. It came to rest only a few feet from where I was hiding.

The giant bird didn't seem to notice that a stone had taken the place of the oval crystal. She settled in her nest and fell asleep.

After a while I crept from my hiding place and retrieved my sword. Now was my chance, I thought. One mighty slash across the peridrone's neck would finish her for good. I quietly approached the nest, raised my sword, and braced myself to strike. But I could not bring myself to wield the fatal blow. I realized I was the intruder here. The peridrone had not sought me out to do me harm. She had only tried to defend her lair. As I watched her sleeping peacefully, I had no desire to kill the last of a species. I was content to let the Giant Peridrone live out her days guarding the egg-shaped stone that would never hatch.

I stole away from the nest and made my way down the mountain. When I caught up with Jonathan, we raced across the desert. As we neared Galwin Forest, we could see the trees were engulfed in a purple glow. We knew Dorinda's powers were growing stronger by the minute. At top speed we rode straight to the spring.

"Make haste!" Melchior called to us. "Bring the crystal to me!"

Jonathan and I leaped from our horses and placed the crystal before Melchior. The Ancient One stretched out both of his hands, and a light of energy began to glow within the oval shape. As we watched, the crystal rose from the ground and became suspended in midair.

"You have completed your task, and you have done well," Melchior said to us. "Now I must do the rest."

"Let me go with you," Olaf said, stepping forward.

"No, old friend," Melchior replied. "I must do this alone.

The wizard grasped the glowing object with his hands and said, "Hear me, Dorinda! Your wickedness will now be stopped!" Then, holding tightly to the crystal, Melchior jumped into the swirling waters.

"Master, wait for me!" Olaf cried out. And before Jonathan and I could hold him back, Olaf the Dwarf threw himself into the spring and followed his master to the spiraling depths.

Lightning flashed and thunder roared. The ground trembled and a spire of water shot upward into the sky. Then, as suddenly as the turmoil had begun, it stopped. The waters fell back and the spring began to bubble sweet and clear. When I turned to look at Jonathan, I was amazed at what I saw. He no longer had the appearance of a beast. Once again he was a man. In our excitement, we jumped and danced about, and we laughed until I thought we would cry.

When we finally settled down, I walked to the spring, knelt down, and peered into its depths. The black hole had disappeared. I saw only my own reflection. I scooped up a handful of water and brought it to my lips. The cool liquid tasted clean and pure. I knew Dorinda's powers had at last been destroyed and that the spring in Galwin Forest was no longer a place to be feared.

Jonathan and I rode to the Castle of Nor and told King Ansel all that had happened. The king was so overjoyed that he declared a day of celebration. The lords and ladies of the castle and all the villagers were invited. And when Jonathan was reunited with his wife and children, there were tears of joy.

Then, before all who were assembled, and with my good friend, Jonathan, standing by my side, King Ansel commanded me to kneel.

"You have proven your courage in the face of grave danger," he said. "And with no thought of gaining riches, you have saved our kingdom from terrible evils. You have also shown great chivalry by helping a friend in need. For these reasons, I dub thee *Sir Miguel.* From this day forward, you will be known as the Knight of Friendship. Rise, Sir Miguel, and walk in peace."

My dream of becoming a knight had been fulfilled.

In the years that have followed, my friendship with Jonathan has remained strong and true. And we have never forgotten the events that led to our meeting or the great sacrifice made by the Ancient One to protect the kingdom. One day each year, we travel together to the spring in Galwin Forest. There in the quiet of the woods, we place a wreath of wildflowers upon the waters in remembrance of Melchior and his faithful servant.

THE NATIONAL WRITTEN & ILLUSTRATED

— THE 1989 NATIONAL AWARD WINNING BOOKS —

Lauren Peters
age 7

Michael Cain
age 11

Amity Gaige
age 16

Dennis Vollmer
age 6

Lisa Gross
age 12

Stacy Chbosky
age 14

Problems at the North Pole — Written & illustrated by Lauren Peters

the Legend of SIR MIGUEL — MICHAEL CAIN

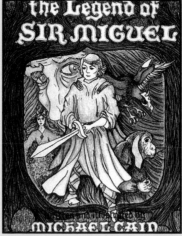

WE ARE A THUNDERSTORM — written and photographed by amity gaige

—THE 1987 NATIONAL AWARD WINNING BOOKS—

JOSHUA DISOBEYS — Written and Illustrated by Dennis Vollmer

THE HALF & HALF DOG — written and illustrated by LISA GROSS

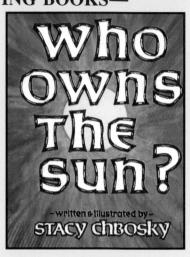

WHO OWNS THE SUN? — written & illustrated by STACY CHBOSKY

—THE 1989 GOLD AWARD WINNERS—

BROKEN ARROW BOY — WRITTEN AND ILLUSTRATED BY ADAM MOORE and his friends

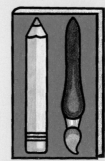

GET THAT GOAT! — WRITTEN AND ILLUSTRATED BY MICHAEL AUSHENKER

Adam Moore
age 9

Michael Aushenker
age 19

Students' Winning Books Motivate and Inspire

Each year it is Landmark's pleasure to publish the winning books of The National Written & Illustrated By... Awards Contest For Students. These are important books because they supply such positive motivation and inspiration for other talented students to write and illustrate books too!

Students of All Ages Love the Winning Books

Students of all ages enjoy reading these fascinating books created by our young author/illustrators. When students see the beautiful books, printed in full color and handsomely bound in hardback covers, they, too, will become excited about writing and illustrating books and eager to enter them in the Contest.

Enter Your Book In the Next Contest

If you are 6 to 19 years of age, you may enter the Contest too. Perhaps your book may be one of the next winners and you will become a published author and illustrator too.